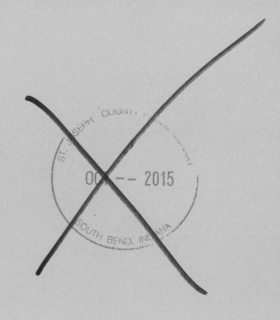

THANKFUL

Eileen Spinelli

Illustrated by
Archie Preston

ZONDERkidz

The waitress is thankful
for comfortable shoes.

The local reporter,
for interesting news.

The gardener's
thankful for
every green
sprout.

The fireman,
for putting the fire out.

The poet is thankful
for words that rhyme.

The children,
for morning
story time.

The artist is thankful

for color and light.

The clown, for her costume

silly and bright.

The doctor is thankful
when patients get well.

The traveler, for a
cozy hotel.

The dancer is thankful.
She loves the beat

that stirs her heart

and hips and feet.

The chef is thankful for
plates licked clean.

The tailor, for her
sewing machine.

The queen is thankful

for afternoon tea.

The beekeeper, for the honey bee.

The mayor is thankful
for every vote.

The sailor, for his sturdy boat.

The birder is thankful
to list a new bird.

The pastor is thankful
for God's loving word.

The crafter is thankful
for glitter and glue.

And me?

I'm ever, so thankful ...

for you!